Out on the Ice in the Middle of the Bay

Story Peter Cumming
Art Alice Priestley

Annick Press, Toronto

Annick Press Ltd.

Annick Press gratefully acknowledges the support of The Canada Council and the Ontario Arts Council.

The author would like to express his appreciation to the Arctic Awareness Program for an opportunity to travel and write on Ellesmere Island.

Canadian Cataloguing in Publication Data

Cumming, Peter, 1951–
    Out on the ice in the middle of the bay

ISBN 1-55037-276-9 (bound) ISBN 1-55037-277-7 (pbk.)

I. Priestley, Alice.   II. Title.

PS8555.U45098 1993   jC813′.54   C92-094639-9
PZ7.C850u 1993

The art in this book was rendered in coloured pencil (layered strokes).
The text has been set in Goudy Old Style by Attic Typesetting.

Distributed in Canada by:
Firefly Books Ltd.
250 Sparks Avenue
Willowdale, Ontario   M2H 2S4

Distributed in the U.S.A. by:
Firefly Books (U.S.) Inc.
P.O. Box 1325
Ellicott Station
Buffalo, New York   14205

 Printed on acid-free paper.

Printed and bound in Canada by
D.W. Friesen & Sons, Altona, Manitoba

For Alexander, my northern bear,
and Mariella, my northern girl

P.C.

For my parents Rosalind and
Leonard

A.P.

On a November afternoon, Leah's mother went visiting, leaving little Leah and her father to look after each other. Leah's father told Leah not to go outside—there were polar bears nearby.

Leah's father lay back on the couch and turned on the TV. His eyes closed. His head nodded. He began to snore.

Leah pulled on her parka. She didn't stop to put on her boots—she crept outside in her sneakers. Quietly, she closed the door behind her.

Snow covered the land. Ice covered the bay. The sun was starting to go down. The moon was coming up. Out on the ice in the middle of the bay, a huge iceberg stood.

On the other side of the iceberg, Mother Nanook, a polar bear, fed Baby Boy Nanook her warm, rich milk. Mother Nanook growled softly, telling her cub not to stray away—there were humans nearby.

Then, Mother Nanook drifted off into a deep, deep sleep.

Baby Nanook was not tired—he was lonely and bored and curious. Baby Nanook wandered away.

The sun was shining red on the snow. The moon was climbing up in the sky. Across the ice from Baby Nanook, an enormous iceberg loomed.

Leah walked away from her house, past the church, down to the beach, and out on the ice towards the iceberg that looked like a magical island of snow.

Baby Nanook sauntered across the ice towards the iceberg that seemed like a giant frozen wall. He lifted his snout, seeking smells from the other side of the iceberg.

Leah's father woke up, and Leah wasn't there.

He looked in the kitchen. He looked in the bathroom. He even looked under her bed. He stuck his head out the door and called "Leah! Leah!" as loud as he could.

He phoned the radio station. "Has anyone seen my little Leah?" he asked.

A teenager phoned in. "I saw a little girl walking past the church," he said.

An old man phoned in. "There are bears. On the ice," he said.

Leah's father grabbed his rifle. He loaded the gun, threw on his parka, and ran out of the house.

Mother Nanook woke, and Baby Nanook wasn't
there. She stood on her hind legs and smelled
the air. She put her head down to the ground.
When she found Baby Nanook's tracks heading
towards the iceberg and the humans beyond—
then she began to run.

Out on the ice in the middle of the bay, Leah was wandering, Baby Nanook was roaming, the sun was sinking, the moon was climbing, the iceberg just standing, when all of a sudden . . .

Little Leah saw Baby Nanook.

Baby Nanook saw little Leah.

Leah's feet were stinging with cold. Baby Nanook looked cuddly and warm, like her toy bear. But *this* bear was big—and *this* bear moved.

Leah walked slowly to the bear.

Baby Nanook cocked his head, studying this curious little walking creature.

Leah reached out and touched Baby Nanook's thick fur, then curled up in a ball at his feet. Baby Nanook crouched down and toyed with Leah, batting her gently back and forth between his paws. Leah snuggled into the warm circle of his chest and legs. Baby Nanook nuzzled her tiny body. He didn't know what to make of her.

Leah's father scrambled over the pressure ice towards the iceberg, his eyes down, desperately seeking Leah's tracks in the shadowy crust of the snow.

Mother Nanook was charging around the end of the iceberg, her nose pressed to the ground, anxiously seeking the scent of her cub.

Leah's father was racing, Mother Nanook was lumbering, the sun was disappearing, the cold moon rising, the iceberg just standing, when all of a sudden . . .

Leah's father saw Mother Nanook—right in front of him!

Mother Nanook saw Leah's father—right in front of her!

Leah's father stopped dead in his tracks. Mother Nanook froze. They stared into each other's eyes.

Mother Nanook reared up on her back legs. Leah's father aimed his rifle at the bear's head. Mother Nanook pulled back her paw to knock off the man's head. Leah's father cocked his gun.

Mother Nanook swung.

Leah's father ducked, and shot.

Mother Nanook missed.

Leah's father, he missed too.

At the explosion from the gun, Leah and Baby Nanook sat bolt upright.

Leah cried out.

Baby Nanook growled.

Leah's father and Mother Nanook whirled around and saw the shadows of their children against the iceberg.

In the heart of Leah's father, a voice rose up, shouting, "Little Leah, child of mine, I never want to see you come to any harm."

In Mother Nanook's heart, a voice welled up crying, "Baby Boy, my flesh, the fat of my milk has carried you through your first winter. Now, stay a winter more with me."

But out on the ice in the middle of the bay, there was only silence in the frozen land. The sun was gone behind black hills that cradled the village. The moon shone cold and clear in the icy sky. The massive iceberg stood, as cold, as hard, as still as a rock.

Then, suddenly, Leah called out and ran to her father. With one hand, Leah's father reached out to grab his daughter. With the other, he kept his rifle pointed at the bears.

Mother Nanook growled, and bounded to Baby Nanook. She nuzzled her son, checking to see that he was safe.

Leah's father pushed Leah behind him. Once again, he took aim at the mother bear. Mother Nanook turned, bared her teeth and hissed.

A chill wind blew over them all.

Mother Nanook growled. Baby Nanook pressed tight up to her and gave a little cry. Leah's father cocked his rifle. Leah reached up and tugged at his sleeve. *"Ataata,"* she whispered. "Father."

And then, on that cold November night, out on the ice in the middle of that bay, under the light of that cold moon, the bear *didn't* attack the man. The man *didn't* shoot the bear.

The bear sidled one step backwards. Then she just stood her ground.

The man took one step back, pushing his daughter behind him. He didn't lower his rifle for a moment.

Then back, back, back stepped Mother and Baby Nanook, towards the iceberg and the sea ice and the floe edge beyond. Back, back, back stepped Leah and her father, back towards their home.

A charcoal cloud passed in front of the moon.

Mother and Baby Nanook spun around and ran to the end of the iceberg. Leah's father shot high over their heads. With a final growl, Mother and Baby Nanook disappeared.

Leah's father lay down his rifle and grabbed Leah up in his arms. For dear life, they hugged each other, listened to each other's wildly beating hearts.

Then, Leah and her father heard a new sound break the stillness of the night. Across the ice, one—no, many—snowmobiles came towards them.

Leah's father hoisted Leah high in the air. Leah waved both arms over her head. The lights came closer, like a New Year's midnight parade.

One light shone ahead of the others.

The first snowmobile roared to a halt. Leah's
mother jumped off and threw her arms around Leah.
"Oh, Leah," she cried. *"Panik.* My daughter!"

The other snowmobiles were arriving. The people
were smiling and quietly laying their hands on
Leah. They were shining their flashlights in the
snow, leaning down and touching the tracks of
the bears and the girl, reading a story in the
tracks, marvelling where Leah and the
bear cub had lain down together.

Then, the snowmobiles started back to the village. On one snowmobile, little Leah sat up front, warming her feet from the heat of the engine. Snug behind her, Leah's mother reached her arms around Leah to drive the snowmobile. Behind her, Leah's father stretched his arms around them both.

Cradled in her parents' arms, Leah felt oh, so wonderfully warm. She was asleep before they got home.

And out on the ice in the middle of the bay?
Out on the ice in the middle of the bay, an iceberg stands. A cold white moon in
a purple sky shines over the silvery snow.

THE END